Essex County Council

Mia the Bridesmaid Fairy was originally published as a
Rainbow Magic special. This version has been specially
adapted for developing readers.

Special thanks to
Rachel Elliot and
Fiona Munro

Reading Consultant: Prue Goodwin, lecturer in literacy and children's books.

ORCHARD BOOKS
338 Euston Road, London NW1 3BH
Orchard Books Australia
Level 17/207 Kent Street, Sydney, NSW 2000

This text first published in 2009 by Orchard Books
This Early Reader edition published in 2014
© 2014 Rainbow Magic Limited.
A HIT Entertainment company. Rainbow Magic
is a trademark of Rainbow Magic Limited.
Reg. U.S. Pat. & Tm. Off. And other countries.

HIT entertainment

Illustrations © Orchard Books 2014

Orchard Books is a division of Hachette Children's Books,
an Hachette UK company

www.hachette.co.uk

# Mia

# the Bridesmaid Fairy

by Daisy Meadows

ORCHARD

www.rainbowmagic.co.uk

The Fairyland Palace

Caribbean Island

Fields

Bella's Wedding Sh

Wedding Shop

Jeweller's

Bickwood

# Story One

## The Silver Sixpence

The Silver Sixpence

"I can't wait for next Saturday!" said Rachel Walker excitedly to her best friend, Kirsty Tate. Esther, Kirsty's cousin, was getting married,

and they were both going to
be bridesmaids!

The girls were staying in
the pretty village of Kenbury,
where the wedding was to take
place. As they stood looking
at the church, they saw people
arriving in their best clothes.

"There must be another
wedding today!" cried Kirsty.

Suddenly, a cream car drew
up, and a smart chauffeur
jumped out and opened the
back door. Inside, the girls
could see a woman wearing a

frothy white dress.

"It's the bride!" Rachel exclaimed. "Isn't she lovely?"

When all the guests had gone into the church, the girls carefully walked across the road to meet Kirsty's aunt at the wedding shop.

"Girls, come and try on your dresses," said Aunt Isabel as soon as they opened the door. Bella, who ran the shop, was holding up two exquisite dresses. The girls gasped in delight.

"Oh, they're beautiful!" Rachel whispered, as they got changed and stood in front of the mirror.

"You both look lovely!" cried Aunt Isabel.

Bella checked the dresses fitted, before the girls got dressed again and began exploring. At the front of the shop was a table filled with wedding accessories, so they dashed over to have a look.

"Look at this tiny bridesmaid figurine!" said Rachel smiling.

"It's glowing!" As the two girls
looked at it, glittering fairy dust
floated down, and in place of
the bridesmaid figurine stood a
sweet little fairy.

"Hello," she said softly. "I'm

Mia the Bridesmaid Fairy!"

The girls were good friends with the Rainbow Magic fairies, and they had often helped them to defeat mean Jack Frost and his naughty goblin servants.

"King Oberon and Queen Titania asked me to sprinkle some of my fairy dust on your dresses," the little fairy went on. "It's my job to make sure all bridesmaids are happy!"

Before the girls could say
anything, the church bells
began to peal. Through the
window they saw the wedding
party posing for a photograph.
Suddenly, a gust of wind blew
the bride's bouquet out of her

hands and towards a muddy puddle! Just in time, Mia sent a jet of sparkling magic from her wand and the bouquet landed softly on the grass. Rachel and Kirsty smiled, but the little fairy looked worried.

"That shouldn't tire me out, but I feel weaker," she sighed. "I wonder if anything is wrong with the wedding charms — the three items that give me my magic powers. Girls, we must go to Fairyland straight away," said Mia.

After letting Kirsty's mum know they'd meet her back at the house, the girls ran from the shop with Mia in Rachel's pocket to find a quiet place. As the fairy waved her wand, a stream of fairy dust shrank the girls to fairy size and whisked them away to Fairyland.

They fluttered down outside the fairy Wedding Workshop.

"This is where we make all sorts of things to help human weddings go smoothly," Mia explained. "It's also where we keep the wedding charms."

But the room was deserted.
"Let's find the king and queen,"
Kirsty suggested. "They'll know
what's happening."

"We're glad to see you, girls," said Queen Titania when they reached the throne room. "These are the other fairies from the workshop."

"Why is it closed, Your Majesties?" asked Rachel.

"Yesterday we held a fairy wedding party," the queen explained, "to thank the fairies for their hard work. But suddenly, Jack Frost appeared with his naughty goblins."

The king carried on with the story.

"The goblins threw cake everywhere and jumped into the chocolate fountain. It was a disaster."

"Then," continued the queen, "Jack Frost stole the wedding charms. We know his goblins have hidden them in the human world."

"We'll help find them!" chorused Rachel and Kirsty.

Mia and the girls rushed back to the human world and were soon fluttering over a small village. Mia explained how one of the charms, the Silver Sixpence, brought prosperity and success to couples.

"Look!" gasped Rachel, pointing at a group of goblins around a wishing well, arguing loudly. "I think they've thrown the Sixpence in!"

Suddenly, one goblin dangled another upside down over the well. Then another went in, and another until there was a chain of goblins trying to reach the Sixpence.

"We have to get

to it first," Kirsty said, flying towards the well.

"I've got an idea!" Rachel cried, suddenly. "Mia, can you create a fake sixpence and confuse the goblins?"

"Yes! Great idea," said Mia as they entered the well nervously. She waved her wand and showed the fake coin to the goblins.

"After her!" they called, as they started

chasing Mia. While all the
goblins were shouting, the girls
picked up Mia's magical coin
from the bottom of the well.

When the goblin finally
snatched the fake coin from
Mia, it disappeared!

The watching goblins were
so surprised they didn't notice
the girls flying away carrying
the real Sixpence!

"It worked like a charm!"
Rachel laughed as they all met
at the top of the
well. With a
touch of her
wand, Mia
returned
the coin to
its Fairyland
size, then
popped it

into a little silk pouch.

"Let's go!" Mia cried as they whizzed back to Aunt Isabel's house and Mia returned the girls to their normal size.

"I'm going to take the Silver Sixpence back to Fairyland to the Wedding Workshop!" Mia said happily. "Thank you so much, girls, and see you soon. We still need to find the other two charms!"

Story Two

The Golden
Bells

The Golden
Bells

Later, Rachel and Kirsty went
to a jewellery shop with Esther.

"Kirsty, look!" exclaimed
Rachel, noticing a velvet pouch
on a table. It was embroidered
with two letters – R and K.

The two friends gasped as
Mia flew out of the small
velvet pouch!

"Hello, girls!" she whispered.

"How are you?" asked Kirsty,
as they quickly moved to a quiet
part of the shop.

"Not great," Mia admitted.
"Things are going wrong for

weddings everywhere! The goblins have taken my magical charm, the Golden Bells, to a Caribbean island!"

"How do you know?" asked Rachel, concerned.

Mia explained that the island was popular for beach weddings, and it was where some of the unluckiest things had been happening.

"The Golden Bells are the charm that controls luck," the little fairy said sadly. "Will you help me look for them?"

"Of course," the girls cried. They told Aunt Isabel they wanted to buy something for the wedding, then rushed outside into a quiet alleyway. Mia shrank them to fairy size and with another flick of her wand, a puffy cloud appeared.

It was shaped like a carriage pulled by four white cloud horses! Mia and the girls climbed in, and were whisked away. During the journey, Mia explained how years before, King Oberon had helped a leprechaun. The leprechaun was so grateful he gave the king two lucky gold bells. "They are the charms that bring luck to all weddings," finished Mia.

"We must find the Golden Bells!" said Rachel. "We can't

let Jack Frost use all that luck."

They felt the carriage sinking lower until they tumbled out onto a sandy beach. The cloud horses pulled the carriage into the air, losing their shape and becoming ordinary clouds.

Mia was looking pale. "I'm feeling weak," she said.

"Don't worry," replied Kirsty. "We'll soon find the Golden Bells and recharge your magic."

The girls gazed at the tall palm trees on the beach waving in the warm breeze.

"Maybe luck is on our side after all!" said Rachel, pointing down the beach.

A group of goblins were playing beach volleyball, and arguing furiously about who was winning. They were

pushing and shoving, and
yelling and kicking.

"That's ten points to us!"
shouted a goblin in a purple
flowery swimming cap.

"No, you're wrong!" snapped
one wearing orange flippers.

The other goblins piled on top of them and Rachel shook her head in amazement. "They must really enjoy squabbling, because they even do it on holiday!" she exclaimed.

Then she gave a gasp and pointed. On a long ribbon, dangling from a nearby palm tree, were the Golden Bells!

The girls and Mia flew up to the tree, staying out of sight. Kirsty and Rachel held their breath as Mia reached towards the bells but suddenly, there was a...THUMP! The volleyball banged against the tree, flinging the Golden Bells into the air, and they landed in the arms of a waiting goblin!

"Fairies!" he shouted, spotting their fluttering wings. He threw a handful of sand at them!

Rachel, Kirsty and Mia squeezed their eyes shut as the sand rained down on them. When they opened them, the goblins had gone.

"They must have run like the wind!" said Kirsty crossly.

Mia and the girls fluttered over trees, peered into caves and flew around rocks and bushes, keeping their eyes peeled for a glint of goblin green or a flash

of gold. But the longer they
looked, the paler Mia became.
Suddenly, Rachel stopped.

"I can hear something!" she
said. "It sounds like goblins!"
They flew around some palm

trees and saw a large pool at the base of a frothing waterfall. And swinging across it on ropes, yelling and screeching, was a gaggle of goblins!

"Whoopee!" yelled the silly green creatures, their excited screeches echoing around the clearing. There were goblins everywhere, but where were the Golden Bells? The girls and Mia fluttered around, taking care to stay out of sight until Kirsty gave a little cry.

"Look!" she said, pointing to

a glint of gold amid the green!
The Golden Bells were hanging
from a high branch, protected
by two goblins. They were
arguing about who was taking
up most room on the branch.

As the girls watched, the silly creatures lost their grip and tumbled from the tree.

"Now's our chance!" Kirsty said, as they quickly fluttered to the branch.

"I'll unhook the Golden Bells!" said Mia, trying to tug the ribbon loose.

"You'll have to be fast!" called Rachel in alarm. "The goblins are climbing back up the tree!"

As the goblins lunged for the branch, they managed to shove

the girls out of their way.

"Help!" cried Kirsty. "I'm falling!" The girls and the goblins lost their balance.

Then they fell towards the ground, in a tangled mass of arms, legs and wings!

They landed on a soft pile
of leaves. There was a tinkle as
the Golden Bells landed nearby,
and Mia grabbed them.

The goblins were furious
as they stomped away, still
shoving and arguing.

Rachel and Kirsty sighed with relief.

"Thank you both so much for helping me find the second wedding charm," Mia said. With a twirl of her wand, she restored the Golden Bells to their Fairyland size and tucked them safely into her dress. She gave another wave of her wand, and Rachel and Kirsty closed their eyes as a whirl of sparkling confetti made them human-sized again. When they opened their eyes, they were in

a quiet road by the jewellery
shop.

"I'm going back to
Fairyland," said Mia happily.

"But I'll see you very soon. We still have to find the third wedding charm – the Moonshine Veil!" The girls were just about to ask Mia more about it, when she disappeared in a flurry of sparkles!

"Hi, girls," Esther called from the doorway of the shop. "Come and help me choose some earrings!"

Rachel and Kirsty hurried inside. There were diamond studs, dangling pendants and pretty flower-shaped earrings.

But Rachel and Kirsty knew exactly which ones to pick. They both pointed at a pair in the shape of tiny, golden bells!

Story Three

The Moonshine Veil

The Moonshine Veil

"One more night to go!" said Kirsty, brushing her hair.

"But we haven't found the Moonshine Veil," Rachel sighed. "And I'm worried about the mischief Jack Frost and his naughty goblins could make at the wedding."

"Let's try not to worry," Kirsty said, opening the window wide. "I'm sure we can help Esther have the perfect day!" Outside, the sky was filled with stars.

"Oh, Kirsty – look!" Rachel pointed up at a shooting star, burning across the sky. "That's funny," she went on. "It isn't fading. It seems to be getting bigger and bigger."

Sure enough, the burning star was becoming brighter and brighter!

"It's coming right at us!" Rachel cried.

They jumped aside and the star shot between them onto the carpet, fizzing and crackling. It was Mia!

"Hello, girls!" she said.
"Will you help me find the
Moonshine Veil?"

"Of course!" said Kirsty and
Rachel at once.

"It's the happiness charm,"
explained Mia. "And this is the
best time to spot it. The veil
glows in the dark, and there's a

lunar eclipse tonight!"

The girls frowned.

"The Earth is going to pass between the moon and the sun," Mia explained, creating a magical picture with her wand. "It will block the sun's light, and the Earth's shadow will cover the moon. The only moonlight will be coming from the Moonshine Veil, making it easy to spot."

Mia swished her wand and shrank the girls to fairy size before they fluttered out of the window into the night.

"How will we know where to look?" asked Kirsty.

"I've got an idea," said Rachel, suddenly. "If Mia can magic up a feast, the goblins are sure to turn up to steal the food! And we will see if they have the Moonshine Veil."

"It's risky, but it might just work," said Mia.

She flicked her wand and a marvellous feast appeared. There were jugs of lemonade, sandwiches and sweet treats.

They hid themselves behind some daisies, and almost straight away heard jabbering voices. A group of goblins walked towards the feast, all carrying rucksacks. One rucksack was glowing silvery-grey!

"Look! The Moonshine Veil!" Kirsty exclaimed.

As the goblins reached for the enchanted food, it all disappeared! Mia, Rachel and Kirsty fluttered from their hiding place towards the goblins.

"Give back the Moonshine Veil!" Mia demanded. "Then we'll give you as many cakes as you can eat."

"You pesky fairies! It's a trick!" said the tallest goblin, his tummy rumbling. "The cakes will disappear just like the feast."

"But I'm really hungry," wailed another goblin. "Just give them the silly veil."

The girls and Mia were so distracted by the squabbling goblins, they didn't notice two of them creeping up and throwing a net over them from behind!

The goblins quickly tied up the net with a rope.

"Oh no!" whispered Mia. "I can't reach my wand!"

"We've tricked the silly fairies!" cackled the tall goblin, and they all ran off.

"Mia, can you magic us out of here?" asked Kirsty.

"Not without my wand," Mia sighed. "But listen!"

They heard a snuffling noise and saw a brown fieldmouse.

"Hello, little mouse! Please can you help us?" called Mia. "We're stuck!"

The little mouse nibbled the net until there was a hole large enough for the friends to clamber through.

"Thank you!" Mia said, picking up her wand, and the

fairies flew away.

"The eclipse is almost complete!" Rachel said as they fluttered into the dark human world. But one street was bathed in light.

"That's where the Moonshine Veil is!" cried Mia, landing outside Bella's wedding shop. It was crawling with

goblins messing around. One, dressed in a pageboy outfit, tripped up another in a pink frilly bridesmaid dress.

Suddenly, Mia waved her wand towards Kirsty.

"What are you doing?" Kirsty asked in a growly whisper.

"Helping you sound scary like Jack Frost!" Mia said. Kirsty nodded.

"Give me the Moonshine Veil NOW!" Kirsty bellowed crossly at the shocked goblins.

Trembling, one of them pulled the shimmering veil from his pocket.

"Put it on the floor!" roared Kirsty. But her voice cracked – the enchantment was wearing off! The goblins spotted the girls and rushed forward.

Hands pulled at the precious Moonshine Veil from all sides.

"Oh no! It's going to tear!" Mia exclaimed.

In despair, the girls let go, the goblins tumbled forwards and the Moonshine Veil went flying into the air.

As Mia darted up and caught it, the sparkly veil shrank back to fairy size.

"Thank you, girls!" Mia said. "Now we must return to Fairyland!" She tucked the veil into her dress and a silvery glow whirled them away.

They landed in the Fairyland Palace, and Mia eagerly produced the Moonshine Veil.

"Well done, all of you!" cried Queen Titania.

They hurried to the Wedding Workshop, where there were three alcoves in the wall. The Silver Sixpence lay in one, the Golden Bells in another.

The centre alcove was empty. Mia laid the Moonshine Veil down and the whole room magically glowed.

"Everything is in its place again," said Mia.

"Now it's time for you to be bridesmaids," said the queen. "Good luck, and thank you!"

The queen waved her wand and Rachel and Kirsty

disappeared in a sparkle of fairy magic.

All at once they were back in their bedroom and human-sized again. It was the morning of the wedding! Kirsty and Rachel put on their lovely dresses and Mrs Tate decorated their hair with tiny pink roses. Esther looked like a princess in her ivory dress.

As the bride and groom stepped out of the church after the ceremony, confetti fluttered around their heads.

"Everyone say 'Cheese'!" called the photographer.

Kirsty and Rachel put their arms around each other's waist and exchanged a secret smile. They had a much better word. "MAGIC!"

**If you enjoyed this story,
you may want to read**

Shannon the Ocean Fairy
Early Reader

**Here's how the story begins...**

Rachel Walker and her best
friend Kirsty Tate raced across
Leamouth Beach, laughing.
They were on holiday together,
staying with Kirsty's gran.

Down where the waves
lapped onto the sand, the girls
noticed a beautiful seashell.
They gasped as a burst of pale

blue sparkles fizzed out of it.

"Fairy magic!" Kirsty whispered. Their friendship with the fairies was a very special secret.

"Hello, girls," said a voice from the shell.

"It's the Fairy Queen!" Rachel grinned.

"We'd like to invite you to a special beach party," said the Queen. "I hope you can come."

Suddenly, a rainbow shot out from the shell. When the two friends stepped onto it, they disappeared in a whirl of fairy magic.

The girls had been magically turned into fairies and were now standing on a different beach. It was crowded with fairies enjoying a party. King Oberon and Queen Titania welcomed them.

"The tide's coming in. Will the party end soon?" Rachel asked a nearby fairy. It was Shannon the Ocean Fairy! She was wearing a pink skirt and had a glittering starfish clip in her hair.

"No. The sea never comes beyond Party Rock," Shannon smiled, pointing to a boulder.

Read
Shannon the Ocean Fairy
Early Reader
to find out
what happens next!

Learn to read with

- Rainbow Magic Early Readers are easy-to-read versions of the original books
- Perfect for parents to read aloud and for newly confident readers to read along
- Remember to enjoy reading together. It's never too early to share a story!

Everybody loves Daisy Meadows!

'I love your books' – Jasmine, Essex

'You are my favourite author' – Aimee, Surrey

'I am a big fan of Rainbow Magic!' – Emma, Hertfordshire

# Meet the first seven Rainbow Fairies

Ruby
the Red
Fairy

Amber
the Orange
Fairy

Saffron
the Yellow
Fairy

Fern
the Green
Fairy

Sky
the Blue
Fairy

Izzy
the Indigo
Fairy

Heather
the Violet
Fairy

There's a fairy book for everyone at:
www.rainbowmagicbooks.co.uk

Become a
Rainbow Magic
fairy friend and be the first to
see sneak peeks of new books.

There are lots of special offers and exclusive
competitions to win sparkly
Rainbow Magic prizes.

Sign up today and receive your
FREE Rainbow Magic Reading Star Chart
www.rainbowmagicbooks.co.uk/newsletter